ONE NIGHT, A GROUP OF NORMANS ON THEIR WAY TO A GREAT TOURNAMENT SOUGHT SHELTER. THEY INCLUDED SIR BRIAN DE BOIS-GUILBERT, A MEMBER OF THE KNIGHTS TEMPLAR, AN ORDER OF KNIGHTS FOUNDED DURING THE CRUSADES.

TELL ME, SLAVE, ARE WE NEAR THE DWELLING OF CEDRIC THE SAXON?

STAY ON THIS PATH TILL YOU COME TO A SUNKEN CROSS. THEN TAKE THE PATH TO THE LEFT.

AS THE NORMANS RODE AWAY...

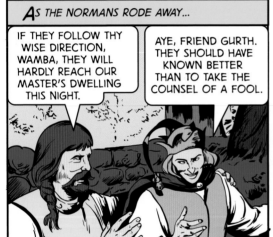

IF THEY FOLLOW THY WISE DIRECTION, WAMBA, THEY WILL HARDLY REACH OUR MASTER'S DWELLING THIS NIGHT.

AYE, FRIEND GURTH. THEY SHOULD HAVE KNOWN BETTER THAN TO TAKE THE COUNSEL OF A FOOL.

LATER...

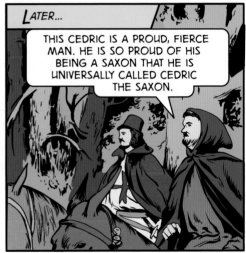

THIS CEDRIC IS A PROUD, FIERCE MAN. HE IS SO PROUD OF HIS BEING A SAXON THAT HE IS UNIVERSALLY CALLED CEDRIC THE SAXON.

I SHALL EXPECT MUCH BEAUTY IN HIS CELEBRATED WARD, ROWENA, TO COUNTERBALANCE THE COMPANY OF SUCH A TRAITOROUS CHURL.

BE CAREFUL OF HOW YOU LOOK ON ROWENA. IT IS SAID CEDRIC BANISHED HIS ONLY SON, WILFRED OF IVANHOE, FOR LOOKING WITH AFFECTION ON HER. NOW IVANHOE FIGHTS WITH KING RICHARD IN THE CRUSADES.

SOON...

HERE IS THE SUNKEN CROSS. HE BID US TURN TO THE LEFT.

TO THE RIGHT, TO THE BEST OF MY REMEMBRANCE.

PERHAPS THAT MAN AT THE FOOT OF THE CROSS CAN TELL US.

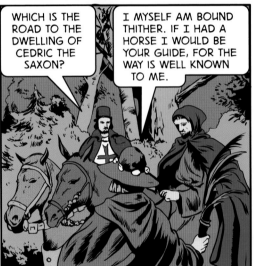

WHICH IS THE ROAD TO THE DWELLING OF CEDRIC THE SAXON?

I MYSELF AM BOUND THITHER. IF I HAD A HORSE I WOULD BE YOUR GUIDE, FOR THE WAY IS WELL KNOWN TO ME.

THE MAN WAS GIVEN A HORSE. HE LED THEM DOWN THE PATH ON THE RIGHT.

WHO AND WHAT ARE YOU?

I AM A PALMER* JUST RETURNED FROM PALESTINE.

*A PILGRIM WHO HAD VISITED VARIOUS SACRED PLACES IN JERUSALEM

A SHORT TIME LATER...

HERE IS THE DWELLING OF CEDRIC THE SAXON.

3

CEDRIC WAS A HOSPITABLE, THOUGH UNWILLING, HOST. HE ASKED ABOUT THE CRUSADES.

WHO NOW BEAR THEMSELVES BEST IN PALESTINE?

THE KNIGHTS TEMPLAR, WHO ARE SWORN TO CHAMPION THE HOLY CROSS.

THEN ROWENA SPOKE.

WERE THERE NONE AMONG THE SAXONS WHOSE NAMES ARE WORTHY TO BE MENTIONED?

THE SAXONS WERE SECOND ONLY TO THE TEMPLARS.

THE PALMER, WHO HAD BEEN SITTING BY THE FIRE, INTERRUPTED.

THE SAXONS WERE SECOND TO NONE. I MYSELF SAW THEE, SIR TEMPLAR, CAST TO THE GROUND BY A SAXON KNIGHT IN A TOURNAMENT.

WHAT WAS THE NAME OF THE GALLANT KNIGHT?

IT WAS THE KNIGHT OF IVANHOE. WERE HE IN ENGLAND NOW, I WOULD CHALLENGE HIM TO MEET ME.

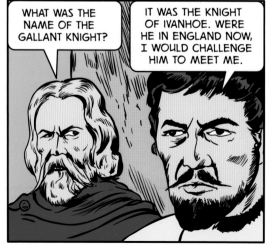

I PROMISE YOU, SIR TEMPLAR, IVANHOE WILL SOMEDAY ACCEPT YOUR CHALLENGE.

AT THAT MOMENT, A NEW GUEST WAS ANNOUNCED.

ISAAC OF YORK, A MERCHANT JEW, SEEKS SHELTER FOR THE NIGHT.

ADMIT HIM, BE HE WHO OR WHAT HE MAY.

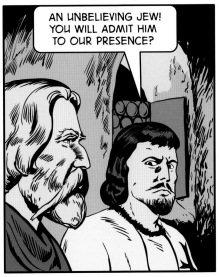

AN UNBELIEVING JEW! YOU WILL ADMIT HIM TO OUR PRESENCE?

MY HOSPITALITY IS NOT BOUNDED BY YOUR DISLIKES.

ISAAC ENTERED. EVEN THE SERVANTS WITHDREW FROM HIM IN PIOUS HORROR.

WHEN THE DINNER WAS OVER, THE TEMPLAR SPOKE TO THE SERVANT.

WHEN THE JEW LEAVES IN THE MORNING, CARRY HIM TO THE CASTLE OF REGINALD FRONT-DE-BOEUF. WE SHALL HAVE RICH RANSOM FOR HIS WORTHLESS SKIN.

EARLY THE NEXT MORNING, THE PALMER SLIPPED INTO ISAAC'S ROOM.

AWAKE, ISAAC. FEAR NOTHING FROM ME. I COME AS YOUR FRIEND.

THE TEMPLAR PLANS TO SEIZE YOU FOR RANSOM. YOU MUST FLEE.

HOLY GOD OF ABRAHAM!

I WILL HELP YOU TO ESCAPE BY GUIDING YOU ALONG THE SECRET PATHS IN THE FOREST. FOLLOW ME.

LATER, WHEN THEY WERE A SAFE DISTANCE FROM THE CASTLE...

THOU HAST SAVED MY LIFE. FOR THAT, I WILL GRANT THEE THY DEAREST WISH, WHICH IS FOR A HORSE AND ARMOUR FOR THE COMING TOURNAMENT.

THOU SPEAKEST TRUE, ISAAC. WHAT FRIEND PROMPTED THAT GUESS?

AS YOU STOOPED OVER MY BED, I SAW THAT THY PALMER'S GOWN HIDES A KNIGHT'S ARMOUR. TAKE THIS NOTE TO MY KINSMAN NEARBY. HE WILL FURNISH THEE FOR THE COMING TOURNAMENT.

THE DAY OF THE GREAT TOURNAMENT AT ASHBY ARRIVED.

AMONG THE SPECTATORS WERE CEDRIC AND ROWENA. WITH THEM WAS ATHELSTANE, A DESCENDANT OF THE LAST SAXON KING OF ENGLAND.

THOUGH ROWENA LOVED IVANHOE, CEDRIC HAD PLEDGED HER TO MARRY ATHELSTANE, WHO CEDRIC HOPED WOULD ONE DAY RULE ENGLAND.

ARE YOU NOT TEMPTED TO JOIN THESE KNIGHTS, MY LORD?

IT IS NOT WORTHWHILE FOR ME.

ISAAC OF YORK WAS ALSO THERE, WITH HIS DAUGHTER, REBECCA.

YONDER JEWESS IS THE VERY MODEL OF PERFECTION!

THE SIGNAL WAS GIVEN FOR THE TOURNAMENT TO BEGIN. FIVE NORMAN KNIGHTS, LED BY SIR BRIAN DE BOIS-GUILBERT, CHALLENGED THE FIELD. FIVE SAXON KNIGHTS ACCEPTED THE CHALLENGE.

AT THE FLOURISH OF TRUMPETS, THEY STARTED OUT AGAINST EACH OTHER AT FULL GALLOP.

THE TEMPLAR AND HIS NORMAN KNIGHTS WERE VICTORIOUS.

A SECOND PARTY OF SAXON KNIGHTS TOOK THE FIELD. BUT THEY, TOO, WERE DEFEATED BY THE NORMANS.

TWICE MORE, THE NORMANS WERE VICTORIOUS.

THE DAY IS AGAINST US.

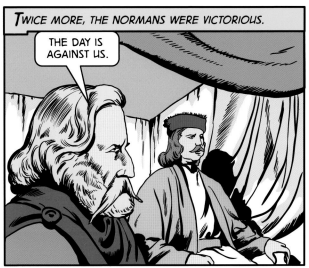

THEN, A SOLITARY TRUMPET ANNOUNCED A NEW OPPONENT.

HIS SHIELD PROCLAIMS HIM TO BE DISINHERITED.

METHINKS IT IS THE YOUNG PALMER WHO SAVED MY LIFE. OUR KINSMAN HATH GIVEN HIM A GOOD HORSE AND NOBLE ARMOUR.

THE DISINHERITED KNIGHT RODE STRAIGHT TO THE TENT OF BOIS-GUILBERT. HE STRUCK THE NORMAN'S SHIELD WITH THE SHARP END OF HIS LANCE.

THE SPECTATORS WERE ASTONISHED AT THE STRANGER'S DARING.

IT IS A CHALLENGE TO MORTAL COMBAT!

ARE YOU SO READY TO DIE, SIR DISINHERITED, THAT YOU PERIL YOUR LIFE SO FRANKLY?

I AM FITTER TO MEET DEATH THAN THOU ART, PROUD NORMAN.

THEN LOOK YOUR LAST UPON THE SUN. THIS NIGHT THOU SHALT SLEEP IN PARADISE.

THE TWO MEN FACED EACH OTHER IN THE LISTS.

WHEN THE TRUMPETS SOUNDED, THEY RODE TOWARDS EACH OTHER.

THEY MET WITH THE SHOCK OF A THUNDERBOLT.

THE DISINHERITED KNIGHT IS TRULY A MATCH FOR BOIS-GUILBERT!

BOTH KNIGHTS RETURNED TO THEIR STATIONS AND RECEIVED FRESH LANCES.

AGAIN THEY MET IN THE CENTRE OF THE FIELD.

THE TEMPLAR IS DOWN!

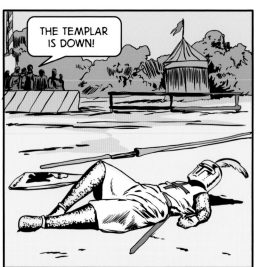

BOIS-GUILBERT, MADDENED BY THE DISGRACE, DREW HIS SWORD.

BUT...

THE COMBAT IS ENDED. SIR DISINHERITED IS DECLARED WINNER OF THE TOURNAMENT. HE MAY NOW CHOOSE A QUEEN OF LOVE AND BEAUTY FOR OUR DAY'S FESTIVAL.

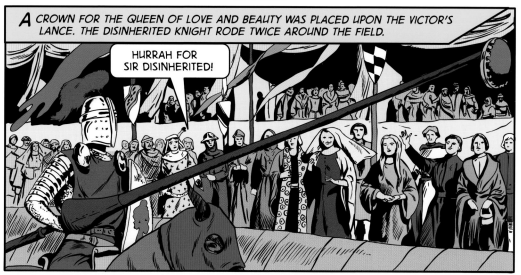

A CROWN FOR THE QUEEN OF LOVE AND BEAUTY WAS PLACED UPON THE VICTOR'S LANCE. THE DISINHERITED KNIGHT RODE TWICE AROUND THE FIELD.

HURRAH FOR SIR DISINHERITED!

THEN HE STOPPED BEFORE ROWENA.

THE CROWN IS YOURS.

HE CHOSE A SAXON QUEEN!

LONG LIVE ROWENA, THE CHOSEN QUEEN OF LOVE AND BEAUTY.

SUDDENLY, THE DISINHERITED KNIGHT FELL SENSELESS.

His helmet was removed.

IVANHOE!

CEDRIC. 'TIS THY SON!

But Cedric refused to acknowledge the banished Ivanhoe.

I HAVE NO SON. LET US GO.

When Cedric's party had gone...

IVANHOE IS WOUNDED. WE MUST TAKE HIM WITH US AND CARE FOR HIM.

AYE, THE GOOD YOUTH MUST NOT DIE.

Rebecca had Ivanhoe placed in her litter.

BUT NOW YOU MUST RIDE EXPOSED TO THE GAZE OF ALL WHO PASS.

And later, Bois-Guilbert twice passed and repassed them, fixing his bold glance on Rebecca.

SHE IS TRULY BEAUTIFUL.

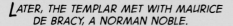

Later, the Templar met with Maurice de Bracy, a Norman noble.

THE SAXON ROWENA IS A FIT QUEEN OF LOVE AND BEAUTY. I WOULD HAVE HER FOR MY WIFE.

HER CHURLISH GUARDIAN, CEDRIC, WOULD NOT HEAR OF IT.

I CARE NOT. I WILL CARRY OFF THE FAIR ROWENA WITHOUT THE CONSENT OF THE BRIDE OR HER FAMILY.

IT IS A NOBLE PLAN, AND GLADLY WILL I AID THEE. CEDRIC AND HIS PARTY MUST PASS THROUGH THE FOREST AS THEY MAKE THEIR WAY BACK TO THEIR DWELLING.

WE WILL TAKE OUR FOLLOWERS, SWOOP DOWN UPON THEM AND CARRY THEM OFF TO THE CASTLE OF REGINALD FRONT-DE-BOEUF, WHERE ROWENA WILL STAY UNTIL SHE BE MY BRIDE.

LET US SET UPON THE PARTY DRESSED AS SAXONS. THE BLAME OF THE VIOLENCE WILL REST WITH THE OUTLAWS OF THE FORESTS.

CEDRIC AND HIS PARTY, UNAWARE OF DE BRACY'S PLAN, MADE THEIR WAY THROUGH THE FOREST. AS THEY JOURNEYED, THEY MET ISAAC AND REBECCA.

OUR SERVANTS HEARD OF A BAND OF OUTLAWS LYING IN WAIT IN THE FOREST. THEY FLED, LEAVING US DEFENCELESS, WITH THE LITTER OF A SICK FRIEND.

WOULD IT PLEASE YOU TO PERMIT US TO TRAVEL UNDER YOUR SAFEGUARD?

THE MAN IS OLD AND FEEBLE, THE MAIDEN YOUNG AND BEAUTIFUL, AND THEIR FRIEND SICK AND IN PERIL OF HIS LIFE. WE CANNOT LEAVE THEM LIKE THIS.

THEY MAY COME WITH US. TAKE UP THE LITTER AND LET US PROCEED.

A SHORT DISTANCE LATER, THEY WERE ATTACKED ON ALL SIDES.

THEY WERE EASY PREY FOR THEIR ASSAILANTS.

ONLY THE TWO SERVANTS, GURTH, THE SWINEHERD, AND WAMBA, THE FOOL, ESCAPED.

WHILE THEY WONDERED WHAT THEY COULD DO, A THIRD PERSON APPEARED.

WHAT IS THE MEANING OF THIS ATTACK? WHO IS IT THAT MAKES PRISONERS IN THESE FORESTS?

METHINKS, SIR OUTLAW, THE FOX SHOULD KNOW HIS CHILDREN. YON VILLAINS WEAR COATS AS LIKE TO THINE AS ONE GREEN PEA POD TO ANOTHER.

I WILL SEE WHO DARES WEAR AN HONEST OUTLAW'S CLOTHING. STIR NOT FROM THE PLACE WHERE YE STAND UNTIL I HAVE RETURNED.

A FEW MINUTES LATER...

I HAVE MINGLED AMONG YON MEN AND HAVE LEARNT THEY BELONG TO MAURICE DE BRACY AND BRIAN DE BOIS-GUILBERT, AND THEY TAKE CEDRIC THE SAXON AND HIS PARTY TO THE CASTLE OF REGINALD FRONT-DE BOEUF.

WE MUST RESCUE OUR MASTER!

FOR THREE MEN TO ATTEMPT IT WOULD BE MADNESS. COME WITH ME UNTIL I GATHER MORE AID.

AFTER SOME TIME, THEY REACHED A SMALL OPENING IN THE FOREST.

STOP!

PUT YOUR BOWS AWAY FOR A BETTER TIME.

IT IS OUR MASTER, ROBIN HOOD.

MEN, HONEST SAXONS HAVE BEEN SEIZED AND CAPTURED IN THESE WOODS. WE MUST PREPARE TO RESCUE THEM.

AYE! AYE!

GO NOW AND SEEK YOUR COMPANIONS. COLLECT WHAT FORCE YOU CAN, AND MEET ME HERE. I GO TO FIND FRIAR TUCK.

ROBIN HOOD WENT TO FRIAR TUCK'S CELL.

OPEN, FRIAR!

FRIAR TUCK OPENED THE DOOR. BEHIND HIM WAS A TALL KNIGHT IN BLACK ARMOUR.

WHO IS THIS KNIGHT?

I AM A GOOD ENGLISHMAN.

I WOULD WILLINGLY BELIEVE SO. HEAR ME, AND I WILL TELL THEE OF AN ENTERPRISE IN WHICH, IF THOU REALLY BE WHAT THOU SEEMEST, THOU MAY TAKE AN HONOURABLE PART.

ROBIN HOOD TOLD THEM OF THE CAPTURE OF CEDRIC'S PARTY BY BOIS-GUILBERT AND DE BRACY.

HAVE SUCH MEN TURNED THIEVES AND OPPRESSORS?

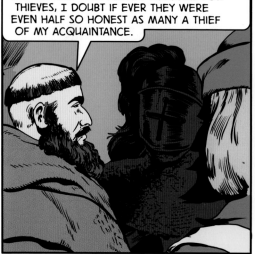

OPPRESSORS THEY ALWAYS WERE. AS FOR THIEVES, I DOUBT IF EVER THEY WERE EVEN HALF SO HONEST AS MANY A THIEF OF MY ACQUAINTANCE.

I WILLINGLY BELIEVE IT. I WILL AID THEE IN SETTING THE CAPTIVES FREE.

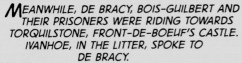

MEANWHILE, DE BRACY, BOIS-GUILBERT AND THEIR PRISONERS WERE RIDING TOWARDS TORQUILSTONE, FRONT-DE-BOEUF'S CASTLE. IVANHOE, IN THE LITTER, SPOKE TO DE BRACY.

IF YOU ARE A SAXON, I PUT MYSELF UNDER YOUR PROTECTION. I AM WILFRED OF IVANHOE.

LATER, AS DE BRACY RODE WITH BOIS-GUILBERT...

THIS FRAY HAS GAINED US GREATER SPOILS THAN WE DREAMT.

TRUE. I NOW HAVE SOMETHING I CAN TERM EXCLUSIVELY MY OWN.

MEANEST THOU THE MONEY OF ISAAC, THE JEW?

HE IS BUT HALF-PRIZE. I MUST SHARE HIS SPOILS WITH FRONT-DE-BOEUF, WHO WILL NOT LEND US THE USE OF HIS CASTLE FOR NOTHING.

NO, HIS DAUGHTER, THE LOVELY JEWESS REBECCA, SHALL BE MY PRIZE.

WHEN THEY REACHED FRONT-DE-BOEUF'S CASTLE, THE CAPTIVES WERE SEPARATED. ISAAC WAS THROWN INTO A DUNGEON, WHERE HE WAS VISITED BY FRONT-DE-BOEUF.

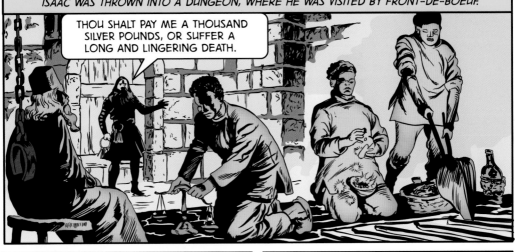

THOU SHALT PAY ME A THOUSAND SILVER POUNDS, OR SUFFER A LONG AND LINGERING DEATH.

ROBBER AND VILLAIN! I WILL PAY THEE NOTHING UNLESS MY DAUGHTER IS RETURNED TO ME IN SAFETY AND HONOUR!

ART THOU MAD? HAS THY FLESH AND BLOOD A CHARM AGAINST HEATED IRON AND SCALDING OIL?

MY DAUGHTER IS DEARER TO ME THAN MY LIMBS, WHICH THY CRUELTY THREATENS.

STRIP HIM AND CHAIN HIM DOWN UPON THE BARS.

JUST THEN, A HORN WAS BLOWN THREE TIMES.

SOMEONE IS AT THE GATE. LET THE DOG BE, FOR NOW. I MUST SEE TO THIS INTRUSION.

WHILE FRONT-DE-BOEUF WAS IN ISAAC'S DUNGEON, MAURICE DE BRACY, NOW IN HIS OWN FINERY, WAS WITH ROWENA.

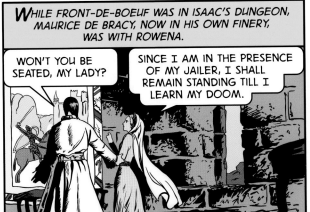

WON'T YOU BE SEATED, MY LADY?

SINCE I AM IN THE PRESENCE OF MY JAILER, I SHALL REMAIN STANDING TILL I LEARN MY DOOM.

FAIR ROWENA, IT IS I THAT AM A PRISONER. I AM CAPTIVE TO THY BEAUTY.

I KNOW YOU NOT, SIR KNIGHT.

I AM MAURICE DE BRACY, AND I TELL THEE THOU SHALT NEVER LEAVE THIS CASTLE, OR THOU SHALT LEAVE IT AS MY WIFE.

THEN I SHALL NEVER LEAVE THIS CASTLE.

DE BRACY GREW ANGRY.

I KNOW YOU LOVE WILFRED OF IVANHOE. BUT KNOW YOU, LADY, THAT HE IS A PRISONER IN THIS CASTLE?

IVANHOE HERE! OH, SAVE HIM! SAVE HIM!

JUST THEN, THE HORN SOUNDED AT THE GATE.

I MUST GO NOW. THINK ON IT - I WILL SAVE IVANHOE IF YOU CONSENT TO BE MY BRIDE. IF YOU DO NOT, HE DIES.

AT THE SAME TIME THAT DE BRACY ENTERED ROWENA'S ROOM, REBECCA'S DOOR OPENED TO ADMIT BOIS-GUILBERT.

TAKE THESE JEWELS AND BE MERCIFUL TO ME AND MY AGED FATHER.

I HAVE MADE A VOW TO PREFER BEAUTY TO WEALTH.

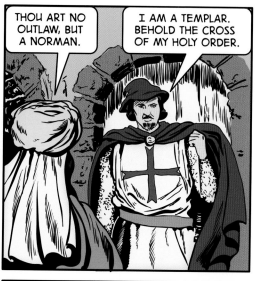

THOU ART NO OUTLAW, BUT A NORMAN.

I AM A TEMPLAR. BEHOLD THE CROSS OF MY HOLY ORDER.

DAREST THOU MENTION IT, WHEN THOU ART ABOUT TO DISHONOUR THY VOWS AS A KNIGHT AND A MAN OF RELIGION?

WELL PREACHED, REBECCA. BUT THOU ART MY CAPTIVE, AND SUBJECT TO MY WILL.

I SPIT AT THEE AND I DEFY THEE!

REBECCA THREW OPEN THE WINDOW AND IN AN INSTANT STOOD ON THE PARAPET WITH NOTHING BETWEEN HER AND THE TREMENDOUS DEPTH BELOW.

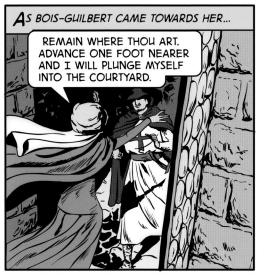

AS BOIS-GUILBERT CAME TOWARDS HER...

REMAIN WHERE THOU ART. ADVANCE ONE FOOT NEARER AND I WILL PLUNGE MYSELF INTO THE COURTYARD.

COME DOWN, RASH GIRL! I SWEAR I WILL OFFER THEE NO OFFENCE.

I WILL NOT TRUST THEE, TEMPLAR.

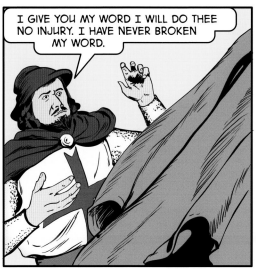

I GIVE YOU MY WORD I WILL DO THEE NO INJURY. I HAVE NEVER BROKEN MY WORD.

REBECCA CAME DOWN, BUT STOOD NEAR THE WINDOW.

THOU NEEDST NO LONGER FEAR ME.

I FEAR THEE NOT, THANKS TO HIM THAT REARED THIS TOWER SO HIGH THAT NONE COULD FALL FROM IT AND LIVE.

REBECCA, MINE THOU MUST BE! BUT IT MUST BE WITH THINE OWN CONSENT AND ON THINE OWN TERMS.

WHEN THE HORN SOUNDED AT THE GATE...

THAT BUGLE ANNOUNCES SOMETHING THAT MAY REQUIRE MY PRESENCE. FAREWELL.

BOIS-GUILBERT, FRONT-DE-BOEUF AND DE BRACY MET IN THE CASTLE HALL.

WHAT IS THE CAUSE OF THIS CURSED CLAMOUR?

A LETTER HATH BEEN DELIVERED ACROSS THE DRAWBRIDGE.

YOU HAVE WRONGFULLY SEIZED CERTAIN PERSONS AND MADE THEM PRISONERS. WE DEMAND THAT THESE PERSONS BE RELEASED OR WE WILL STORM THE CASTLE.

WAMBA, THE FOOL
GURTH, THE SWINE-HERD
THE BLACK KNIGHT
ROBIN HOOD

THESE FELLOWS WOULD NOT DARE ACT WITH SUCH IMPUDENCE IF THEY WERE NOT STRONGLY SUPPORTED.

THERE ARE AT LEAST 200 MEN ASSEMBLED IN THE WOODS, AND MORE ARE COMING.

YOU COULD SEND FOR HELP, BUT THE MESSENGER WOULD BE SET UPON IN THE FOREST.

I HAVE IT. WE WILL ANSWER THE CHALLENGE BY SAYING WE WILL EXECUTE THE PRISONERS. WE WILL ASK FOR A PRIEST FOR THEM. WHEN THE PRIEST ARRIVES, WE CAN SEND HIM WITH OUR MESSAGE FOR AID.

THE CHALLENGE WAS ANSWERED SOON...

I HAVE COME HITHER TO CONFESS THE PRISONERS.

LET HIM CARRY THE MESSAGE FOR AID. BUT SO HE WILL SUSPECT NOTHING, PERMIT HIM TO CONFESS THE SAXON HOGS.

IT SHALL BE SO.

IN CEDRIC'S CELL, THE FRIAR REMOVED HIS FROCK.

WAMBA!

AYE, MASTER, IT IS YOUR TRUSTY SLAVE AND JESTER.

TAKE THOU THIS FROCK AND CORD AND MARCH QUIETLY OUT OF THE CASTLE. YOUR PRESENCE WILL ENCOURAGE OUR FRIENDS TO OUR RESCUE.

IS THERE ANY PROSPECT, THEN, OF RESCUE?

FIVE HUNDRED MEN NOW WAIT WITHOUT.

THEN I GO. WE SHALL FIND THE MEANS OF SAVING YE.

As CEDRIC MADE HIS WAY THROUGH THE CASTLE HALLS...

THOU ART CEDRIC THE SAXON! DENY IT NOT.

IT MATTERS NOT WHO I AM. WHO ARE YOU?

I AM ULRICA, A SAXON. THE FATHER OF FRONT-DE-BOEUF CAPTURED THIS CASTLE FROM MY FATHER.

SINCE THEN I HAVE DWELT IN THESE HALLS – SCORNED AND INSULTED. I HAD NOT THE COURAGE TO DIE, WHICH YOUR PRESENCE NOW GIVES ME.

THERE IS A FORCE WITHOUT THIS CASTLE. LEAD THEM TO THE ATTACK. WHEN THOU SHALT SEE A RED FLAG WAVE FROM THE EASTERN TURRET, PRESS THE NORMANS HARD! I WILL GIVE THEM MUCH TO WORRY THEM FROM WITHIN.

NOW BEGONE, AND LEAVE ME TO MY FATE.

CEDRIC WAS ALSO STOPPED BY FRONT-DE-BOEUF, WHO GAVE HIM THE MESSAGE REQUESTING AID.

CARRY THIS SCROLL TO THE CASTLE OF PHILIP DE MALVOISIN.

YOUR COMMANDS SHALL BE OBEYED.

AS SOON AS CEDRIC JOINED THE BESIEGING FORCES, THE ATTACK ON TORQUILSTONE BEGAN.

THE WHIZZING OF SHAFTS AND MISSILES ON BOTH SIDES WAS INTERRUPTED ONLY BY THE SHOUTS OF THE MEN.

THE BLACK KNIGHT LED THE ATTACK ON THE BARRIERS.

FRONT-DE-BOEUF HEADED THE DEFENDERS.

FRONT-DE-BOEUF AND THE BLACK KNIGHT FOUGHT HAND TO HAND.

THE BLACK KNIGHT FELL, HIS SWORD BROKEN.

IN A MOMENT, HE WAS ON HIS FEET. HE SNATCHED AN AXE AND...

FRONT-DE-BOEUF FELL, MORTALLY WOUNDED.

THE ASSAILANTS WON THE BARRIERS. THEY PRESSED ON TO THE OUTER WALLS.

THE BLACK KNIGHT SPLINTERED THE POSTERN WITH HIS AXE.

THE OUTWORKS WERE WON. NOW ONLY THE MOAT SEPARATED THEM FROM THE CASTLE.

SEE, THEY HAVE DESTROYED THE BRIDGE.

THE BLACK KNIGHT HAD THE MEN BUILD A FLOATING BRIDGE TO CROSS THE MOAT.

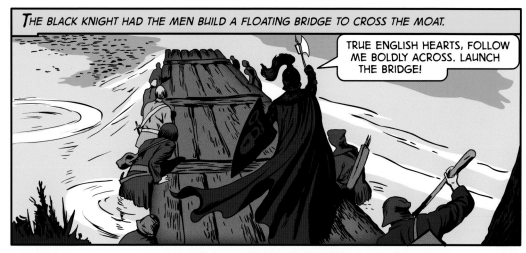

TRUE ENGLISH HEARTS, FOLLOW ME BOLDLY ACROSS. LAUNCH THE BRIDGE!

THE BRIDGE WAS THRUST FORWARDS. THE BLACK KNIGHT AND CEDRIC CROSSED SAFELY, BUT THOSE WHO FOLLOWED WERE INSTANTLY SLAIN, AND THE OTHERS RETREATED.

THE BLACK KNIGHT THUNDERED UPON THE GATE OF THE CASTLE WITH HIS AXE...

WHILE ABOVE HIS HEAD, DE BRACY SOUGHT TO LOOSEN A STONE WHICH WOULD CRUSH HIM AND CEDRIC.

JUST THEN, ULRICA RAISED THE RED FLAG.

SEE YONDER FLAG! IT IS THE APPOINTED SIGNAL WHICH CEDRIC SPOKE OF. IT MEANS THE NORMANS ARE BESIEGED FROM WITHIN AS WELL AS WITHOUT.

AT THE SAME MOMENT, BOIS-GUILBERT LEARNED OF THE NEW DANGER.

ALL IS LOST. SOMEONE HAS SET FIRE TO THE CASTLE.

THOU ART MAD TO SAY SO!

NAY, THE WESTERN SIDE IS ALL IN FLAMES.

WHAT IS TO BE DONE?

LEAD THY MEN DOWN. WE SHALL DEFEND OURSELVES UNTIL THEY GRANT US FAIR QUARTER.

DE BRACY AND HIS MEN RUSHED DOWN TO THE GATE AND THREW IT OPEN. DE BRACY HIMSELF FOUGHT WITH THE BLACK KNIGHT.

THEY DEALT EACH OTHER FURIOUS BLOWS. FINALLY...

YIELD, DE BRACY.

I WILL NOT YIELD TO AN UNKNOWN CONQUEROR.

THE KNIGHT SPOKE HIS NAME SOFTLY...

YOU!

I YIELD AS THY PRISONER, AND I WILL TELL THEE WHAT THOU WOULD WISH TO KNOW.

WILFRED OF IVANHOE IS WOUNDED AND A PRISONER HERE, AND WILL PERISH IN THE BURNING CASTLE IF HE IS NOT RESCUED.

SHOW ME HIS CHAMBER!

AT THAT MOMENT, IVANHOE WAS NOT ALONE. ULRICA HAD LET REBECCA INTO HIS CHAMBER TO CARE FOR HIM IN HIS ILLNESS.

FLY, REBECCA, AND SAVE THINE OWN LIFE. NOTHING CAN HELP ME.

I WILL NOT FLY! WE WILL BE SAVED OR PERISH TOGETHER.

SUDDENLY THE DOOR BURST OPEN...

I HAVE FOUND THEE, REBECCA! THERE IS BUT ONE PATH TO SAFETY. I HAVE CUT MY WAY THROUGH FIFTY DANGERS TO POINT IT OUT TO THEE. FOLLOW ME.

I WILL NOT FOLLOW THEE. RATHER WILL I PERISH IN THE FLAMES THAN ACCEPT SAFETY FROM THEE!

THOU SHALT NOT CHOOSE.

HE SEIZED HER AND BORE HER OFF.

SET HER FREE! VILLAIN, I WILL HAVE THY HEART'S BLOOD!

A FEW MOMENTS LATER, THE BLACK KNIGHT RESCUED IVANHOE.

IF THOU BE A TRUE KNIGHT, THINK NOT OF ME. SAVE REBECCA! SAVE THE LADY ROWENA!

IN THEIR TURN, BUT THINE IS FIRST.

ROWENA, ATHELSTANE, WAMBA AND ISAAC WERE ALSO RESCUED.

BUT BOIS-GUILBERT RODE OFF WITH REBECCA.

THE FIRE WAS SPREADING RAPIDLY THROUGH THE CASTLE WHEN ULRICA, WHO STARTED IT, APPEARED ON A TURRET SINGING A WILD SAXON SONG.

VENGEANCE HATH BUT AN HOUR, I ALSO MUST PERISH!

THE TOWERING FLAMES NOW ROSE TO THE SKIES. ULRICA WAS FOR A LONG TIME VISIBLE ON THE TURRET. THEN IT GAVE WAY, AND SHE PERISHED IN THE FLAMES WHICH CONSUMED THE CASTLE.

Later...

MY THANKS, ROBIN HOOD, TO THEE AND THY BOLD MEN FOR THE LIFE AND HONOUR YOU HAVE SAVED.

NAY! WE DID BUT HALF THE WORK.

IF THE NORMANS DRIVE YE FROM THESE WOODS, REMEMBER I HAVE FORESTS OF MY OWN WHERE YE MAY RANGE IN FREEDOM.

THANKS, GENTLE LADY.

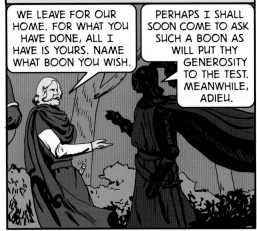

CEDRIC EXPRESSED HIS GRATITUDE TO THE BLACK KNIGHT.

WE LEAVE FOR OUR HOME. FOR WHAT YOU HAVE DONE, ALL I HAVE IS YOURS. NAME WHAT BOON YOU WISH.

PERHAPS I SHALL SOON COME TO ASK SUCH A BOON AS WILL PUT THY GENEROSITY TO THE TEST. MEANWHILE, ADIEU.

AFTER CEDRIC'S PARTY HAD GONE, ISAAC ALSO APPEARED TO LEAVE.

METHINKS THY DAUGHTER WAS CARRIED OFF TO THE TEMPLARS' CASTLE, TEMPLESTOWE. I CANNOT HELP THEE, FOR THE TEMPLARS' LANCES ARE TOO STRONG FOR MY ARCHERS.

BUT I WILL GIVE THEE GUIDES TO LEAD THEE THERE TO PLEAD FOR THE SAFE DELIVERY OF THY CHILD.

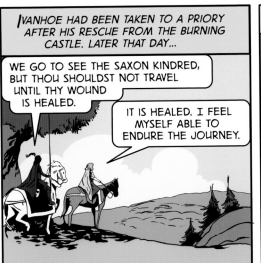

IVANHOE HAD BEEN TAKEN TO A PRIORY AFTER HIS RESCUE FROM THE BURNING CASTLE. LATER THAT DAY...

WE GO TO SEE THE SAXON KINDRED, BUT THOU SHOULDST NOT TRAVEL UNTIL THY WOUND IS HEALED.

IT IS HEALED. I FEEL MYSELF ABLE TO ENDURE THE JOURNEY.

AS THEY ENTERED THE CASTLE...

WRAP THY MANTLE AROUND THY FACE. DO NOT PRESENT THYSELF TO THY FATHER YET.

WHEN THEY STOOD BEFORE CEDRIC...

YOU PROMISED FOR THE SERVICE I RENDERED YOU TO GRANT ME A BOON.

IT IS GRANTED BEFORE IT IS ASKED.

FIRST, LET ME TELL YOU WHO I AM. YOU HAVE KNOWN ME ONLY AS THE BLACK KNIGHT.

KNOW ME NOW AS RICHARD, KING OF ENGLAND.

NOW TO MY BOON. I REQUIRE OF THEE, AS A MAN OF THY WORD, TO FORGIVE THE GOOD KNIGHT, WILFRED OF IVANHOE.

MY FATHER! GRANT ME THY FORGIVENESS!

THOU HAST IT, MY SON.

THEN ATHELSTANE SPOKE.

CEDRIC, THE LADY ROWENA CARES NOT FOR ME. SHE LOVES IVANHOE. I RENOUNCE MY CLAIM TO HER IN FAVOUR OF IVANHOE.

AND HE LED ROWENA TO IVANHOE.

MEANWHILE, ISAAC HAD ARRIVED AT TEMPLESTOWE TO FIND BOIS-GUILBERT. INSTEAD, HE WAS TAKEN BEFORE THE GRAND MASTER OF THE TEMPLARS.

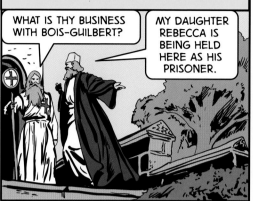

WHAT IS THY BUSINESS WITH BOIS-GUILBERT?

MY DAUGHTER REBECCA IS BEING HELD HERE AS HIS PRISONER.

THE GRAND MASTER WAS FURIOUS.

THROW THIS MAN OUT! SHOOT HIM DEAD IF HE COMES AGAIN!

THEN HE SENT FOR THE PRESIDENT OF TEMPLESTOWE.

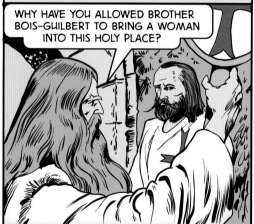

WHY HAVE YOU ALLOWED BROTHER BOIS-GUILBERT TO BRING A WOMAN INTO THIS HOLY PLACE?

THE PRESIDENT SAW THAT HE AND BOIS-GUILBERT WOULD BE RUINED UNLESS HE COULD EXPLAIN.

IF I HAVE SINNED IN RECEIVING HER HERE, IT WAS IN THE ERRING THOUGHT THAT I MIGHT THUS BREAK OFF OUR BROTHER'S WILD AND UNNATURAL DEVOTION TO HER.

I THINK THIS WOMAN IS A SORCERESS. SHE HATH BEWITCHED OUR BROTHER BOIS-GUILBERT.

A SORCERESS! THE WITCH MUST BE JUDGED AND CONDEMNED! PREPARE THE CASTLE HALL FOR THE TRIAL.

THE PRESIDENT HURRIED AWAY TO SEEK BOIS-GUILBERT. HE MET HIM COMING FROM REBECCA'S ROOM.

I SAVED HER LIFE. I WAS THE BUTT OF A HUNDRED ARROWS, BUT I ONLY USED MY SHIELD TO PROTECT HER. THUS DID I ENDURE FOR HER AND NOW SHE UPBRAIDS ME THAT I DID NOT LEAVE HER TO PERISH.

I THINK I WAS RIGHT WHEN I TOLD THE MASTER SHE HATH CAST A SPELL OVER YOU.

HAVE YOU TOLD HIM THAT REBECCA IS HERE?

I COULD NOT HELP IT – HE KNEW ALREADY. BUT YOU ARE SAFE IF YOU RENOUNCE REBECCA. HE BELIEVES SHE IS A SORCERESS AND MUST SUFFER AS SUCH.

SHE SHALL NOT!

SHE MUST AND WILL. NEITHER YOU NOR ANYONE ELSE CAN SAVE HER. I GO NOW TO ORDER THE HALL PREPARED FOR TRIAL.

REBECCA WAS TRIED AND QUICKLY CONDEMNED TO BE BURNED AS A WITCH.

THERE IS YET ONE CHANCE OF LIFE LEFT TO ME. I CHALLENGE THE PRIVILEGE OF TRIAL BY COMBAT.

UNDER TRIAL BY COMBAT, REBECCA COULD DEMAND A CHAMPION TO ENGAGE IN COMBAT WITH A TEMPLAR. IT WAS BELIEVED THAT DURING THE BATTLE, GOD WOULD AID THE JUST CAUSE. IF REBECCA'S CHAMPION WON, IT WOULD MEAN SHE WAS INNOCENT.

I WILL BE REBECCA'S CHAMPION!

BUT...

BROTHER BOIS-GUILBERT, THOU WILT DO BATTLE FOR THE TEMPLARS. WE DOUBT NOT BUT THAT RIGHT WILL TRIUMPH.

REBECCA WAS GIVEN THREE DAYS TO FIND A CHAMPION.

GOD WILL RAISE ME UP A CHAMPION. I PUT MY TRUST IN HIM.

AND REBECCA SENT A MESSAGE TO HER FATHER TELLING HIM WHAT HAD HAPPENED.

THERE IS BUT ONE WHO MIGHT BEAR ARMS IN REBECCA'S BEHALF.

THE DAY FOR THE TRIAL BY COMBAT ARRIVED. REBECCA WAS TAKEN TO A CHAIR NEAR THE STAKE.

BOIS-GUILBERT RELUCTANTLY TOOK HIS PLACE IN THE LISTS.

HERE STANDETH THE GOOD KNIGHT BRIAN DE BOIS-GUILBERT, READY TO DO BATTLE WITH ANY KNIGHT WHO WILL DEFEND REBECCA.

THE TRUMPETS SOUNDED BUT NO CHAMPION APPEARED.

WE WILL WAIT UNTIL THE SHADOWS BE CAST FROM THE WEST TO THE EASTWARD. IF NO CHAMPION APPEARS, REBECCA WILL DIE.

BOIS-GUILBERT RODE TO REBECCA'S SIDE.

MOUNT THEE BEHIND ME ON MY STEED, AND WE WILL FLY FROM THIS PLACE.

TEMPTER, BEGONE!

AS THE TIME PASSED, NO ONE BELIEVED A CHAMPION WOULD APPEAR FOR REBECCA. SUDDENLY...

A CHAMPION! A CHAMPION!

BUT THE KNIGHT'S HORSE APPEARED TO REEL FROM FATIGUE, AND THE RIDER, EITHER FROM WEAKNESS OR WEARINESS, SEEMED SCARCE ABLE TO SUPPORT HIMSELF IN THE SADDLE.

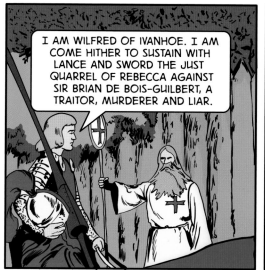

I AM WILFRED OF IVANHOE. I AM COME HITHER TO SUSTAIN WITH LANCE AND SWORD THE JUST QUARREL OF REBECCA AGAINST SIR BRIAN DE BOIS-GUILBERT, A TRAITOR, MURDERER AND LIAR.

I WILL NOT FIGHT WITH THEE AT PRESENT. GET THY WOUNDS HEALED, AND GET THEE A BETTER HORSE.

PROUD TEMPLAR, HAST THOU FORGOTTEN THAT TWICE DIDST THOU FALL BEFORE THIS LANCE? REMEMBER THY PROUD BOAST IN MY FATHER'S HOUSE THAT THOU WOULDST DO BATTLE WITH ME?

DOG OF A SAXON! PREPARE FOR THY DEATH!

THE TWO KNIGHTS TOOK THEIR PLACES. THE TRUMPETS SOUNDED, AND THEY CHARGED.

THE WEARIED HORSE OF IVANHOE, AND ITS NO LESS EXHAUSTED RIDER, WENT DOWN.

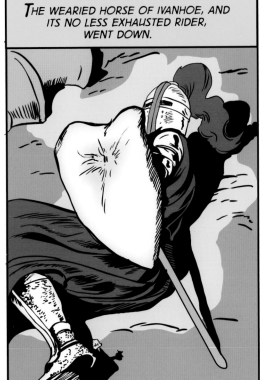

BUT BOIS-GUILBERT, THOUGH HE HAD BARELY BEEN TOUCHED, ALSO FELL.

IN A MOMENT...

YIELD OR DIE.

BUT THE TEMPLAR DID NOT ANSWER.

HE IS DEAD!

THIS IS INDEED THE JUDGEMENT OF GOD. I PRONOUNCE REBECCA FREE AND GUILTLESS.

SOME TIME LATER, REBECCA AND ISAAC LEFT ENGLAND. REBECCA SPENT THE REST OF HER LIFE IN GOOD WORKS – TENDING THE SICK, FEEDING THE HUNGRY AND RELIEVING THE DISTRESSED.

AND IVANHOE AND ROWENA WERE MARRIED. KING RICHARD HIMSELF ATTENDED, AS WELL AS BOTH NORMANS AND SAXONS. IT WAS THE SIGN OF THE FUTURE PEACE AND HARMONY THAT WOULD EXIST BETWEEN THE TWO RACES.

THE END

NOW THAT YOU HAVE READ THE CLASSICS ILLUSTRATED EDITION, WHY NOT GO ON TO READ THE ORIGINAL VERSION TO GET THE FULL ENJOYMENT OF THIS CLASSIC WORK?

Sir Walter Scott (1771-1832)

At the peak of his career, Sir Walter Scott was the most popular writer of his day. His works were so impatiently awaited in the USA that the first sheets of each novel were rushed into print in Philadelphia, Pennsylvania while the last pages were being finished in Edinburgh, Scotland. Then the first batch of 2,000 copies was rushed on horseback from Philadelphia to New York a scarce thirty-six hours after the printer had received the last sheet!

Scott was a sensation, not only in America, but all over Europe. It was said that in Berlin, Germany everyone went to bed with *Waverley* under the pillow and read *Rob Roy* while sipping the morning chocolate.

This literary lion was born in Edinburgh in 1771. When he was eighteen months old, he suffered an attack of polio and lost the use of his right leg. Scott's parents sent him to his grandfather's home to recover. One of Scott's earliest recollections of childhood was lying on the floor in the skin of a freshly killed sheep, being coaxed by his grandfather to crawl.

In spite of his handicap, Scott spent much time outdoors and he grew to be physically active and able. When he was fifteen, he was apprenticed to his father, an attorney. He himself became a lawyer at the age of twenty-one. It was at this time that Scott, whom the law interested very little, began to divide his life into distinct halves. There was a place for business and there was a place for the creative work he enjoyed.

At the age of twenty-six, Scott met and married a French girl, Charlotte Charpentier. Shortly afterwards, he began to publish his poetry.

As time passed, Scott acquired various political and judicial appointments which provided him with an income and left him time to write. His first novel, *Waverley*, was published in 1814. A number of books soon followed, including *Guy Mannering* (1815) and *Rob Roy* (1817). In 1820, his greatest success, *Ivanhoe*, appeared. Scott's novels immediately became the rage the world over. They had romance, action, and were able to present dry historical events in terms of living human beings, Actually, Scott was the father of the modern historical novel.

In 1820, Scott was dubbed Sir Walter. The writer was enchanted by royalty, and when King George IV of England visited Scotland in 1822, Scott was on the welcoming committee. At one point, the King, delighted by Scott's wit, called for brandy to drink his health. Sir Walter, thrilled by this honour, asked that the King's glass be given him as a souvenir of the occasion. Scott reverently wrapped the glass in a kerchief and put it into his back pocket. Some time later, he sat down heavily on a chair. He rose immediately with a scream!

When not writing, Scott's major interest was his estate, Abbotsford. It was a hundred acre tract of land on the Tweed River, and from time to time Scott added to it until it was one of the largest in the countryside. But his dreams of living in his castle, as a feudal knight out of *Ivanhoe*, perhaps, were not to be fulfilled, for Abbotsford was his downfall. He spent wildly for improvements and when, in 1826, a publishing company in which he had a major interest collapsed, Scott went bankrupt.

Sir Walter spent the rest of his life working to pay his creditors. In less than two years after the bankruptcy, Scott published six books, including *The Life of Napoleon Bonaparte* in nine volumes (1827). Scott worked at a feverish pace. The strain wore him down and his health declined rapidly. In 1832, Sir Walter died at Abbotsford.